I shoot my arrows straight and sure,
And rob the rich to help the poor!

I'm a pirate, full of swagger.
Peter Pan must dodge my dagger!

I scrub and clean 'til I have blisters.
How I hate my ugly sisters!

I'm no ogre (that's plain mean talk!) –
Just a giant, up a beanstalk.

I walk the woods all dressed in red –
To visit Granny ill in bed!

I am the fairest of them all.
The mirror said so, on the wall!

A witch has got me in her power.
Someone save me from this tower!

When those three pigs come into town
I'm gonna blow their houses down!

For Jack, with love.
To Islington Writers for Children,
who help stories happen: Thank you – M.R.

For Mum and Dad – E.E.

Captain Hook drawn from Peter Pan by kind permission of
Great Ormond Street Hospital for Children, with thanks.

ORCHARD BOOKS
96 Leonard Street, London EC2A 4XD
Orchard Books Australia
32/45-51 Huntley Street, Alexandria, NSW 2015
First published in Great Britain in 2003
First paperback publication in 2004
ISBN 1 84362 209 2 (hardback)
ISBN 1 84362 417 6 (paperback)
Text © Marion Rose 2003
Illustrations © Edward Eaves 2003
The right of Marion Rose to be identified as the author
and of Edward Eaves to be identified as the illustrator
of this work has been asserted by them in accordance
with the Copyright, Designs and Patents Act 1988.
A CIP catalogue record for this book is available from the British Library.
(hardback) 10 9 8 7 6 5 4 3 2 1
(paperback) 10 9 8 7 6 5 4 3 2 1
Printed in China

Fairy Tale Secrets

Marion Rose

Illustrated by Edward Eaves

ORCHARD BOOKS

Pssst! Do you want to know a secret?
Can you keep it to yourself?
When you're sure there's no-one looking
Sneak this book down from the shelf.

High up in that lonely tower
With no friends for company.
What a sad and lonely lifestyle!
How unhappy she must be.

But, could it be there's something buried
In Rapunzel's sea of hair . . .

Listen! Hear that gentle ring tone?
Look what she's got hidden there!

Robin Hood's a dashing hero,
Riding fast and shooting straight.
Always full of strength and daring.
Small boys think he's really great!

But, if they tailed him to his tree house
They might learn a thing or two...

When the Merry Men aren't looking
This is what he loves to do!

Did you see a flash of scarlet?
Someone running through the trees?
Red Riding Hood is off to Grandma's
With her bag of picnic tea.

But, tiptoe with me very softly.
Do not make a sound! And then...

You might spy a different meeting
In a secret woodland glen!

You may know Jack's thrilling story –
How he climbed the beanstalk high,
Sneaked into the Giant's hallway
In his castle in the sky.

But, when that Giant isn't roaring:
"I smell blood, FEE FI FO FUM"...

cluck!

He spends all his spare time bouncing
On his great, ginormous bum!

Cinderella does the cleaning,
Dusts the shelves and scrubs the floor.
All her clothes are old and ragged.
Everybody knows she's poor.

But, round her neck she wears a ribbon.
Threaded on it is the key...

To a box her own mum left her.
See what's in it? Gracious me!

He's so wonderfully wicked.
He's so good at being bad!
He loves chasing Little Piggies –
Isn't Wolf a rotten cad?

But, there is something he's afraid of –
One thing fills him full of fear...

See what makes him gasp and tremble?
Being tickled under here!

Ha ha h.

Captain Hook's a famous pirate,
Feared across the seven seas.
When they see his awful cruelty,
Strong men fall upon their knees.

But, sneak a look into his cabin
In the fading sunset light…

Please come to my
secret party.
I`ll let down my hair
at midnight.
Love Rapunzel xxx

You will see his best-kept secret
Tucked up with him every night!

Seven shirts she has to iron.
Seven beds she has to make.
Snow White dusts and cleans and tidies –
Never, ever gets a break.

But, if you creep down to the woodshed
In the evening after dark...

There you'll find her secret passion.
What a lady! What a lark!

Psst! Do you have a little secret
That you'd really like to share?
Perhaps you've got a hidden treasure
Or an undiscovered lair?

If you wish to tell your story
We all know what 'hush-hush' means...

Join our secret midnight party
And we'll help you spill the beans!

So, farewell from the forest green
And please don't tell what you have seen!

If you should talk, I'll be quite frank,
I'll make you walk the bloomin' plank!

I'm sure my secret's safe with you.
I'm rich in love – hope you are too!

If you betray me (just like Jack)
I'll have you for my morning snack!

You know what's in my woodland den...
I hope you'll visit us again!

Goodbye! Don't tell the wicked queen
What you know or where you've been!

I'm sorry that you have to go.
I did enjoy our secrets so!

Psst! Don't gossip willy-nilly,
You could make me look quite silly!